P9-CCG-460

A Gift From/Un regalo de:

Windham
School Readiness Council
860.465.3009

The
Beetle Bush

The Beetle Bush

by
Beverly Keller
illustrated by
Marc Simont

COWARD, McCANN & GEOGHEGAN, INC.

New York

Library of Congress Cataloging in
Publication Data

Keller, Beverly
THE BEETLE BUSH
A Break-Of-Day Book

SUMMARY: A little girl is convinced she is a
failure at everything she tries until she begins a
garden.
  [1. Gardening—Fiction] I. Simont, Marc. II.
Title
PZ7.K2813Be3   [E]   75-28180
SBN: GB-698-30618-X   TR-698-20366-6

Printed in the United States of America
07210

For my daughters—my teachers

Arabelle Mott had the grumps.
"I can't do anything right,"
she grumbled.
"When I paint a flower,
everybody asks,
'What's that supposed to be?'

7

When I sing a song,
everybody asks,
'*What's that supposed to be?*'
When I turn a cartwheel,
everybody asks,
'*What's that supposed to be?*'

Arabelle handed her mother
a sheet of paper.
Her mother looked at it.
"What's this supposed to be?"

Arabelle scrunched up her face,
but she did not scream.
"It's a poem.
It tells how I feel."

Mrs. Mott
looked at the paper
again.
"All this says is,
'My life is pale and stale. Your
daughter is a failure.'"

"That's how I feel,"
said Arabelle.

Her mother was worried.
"You're too young
to be a failure.
Why don't you
bake a cake, instead?"
"I'll try anything," Arabelle said.

She sifted the flour
and beat the eggs
and poured the batter
into a pan.
Her mother put the pan
in the oven.

While they were
cleaning up the kitchen,
the doorbell rang.
Mrs. Mott went to answer it.

"Be sure to watch the cake,"
she told Arabelle.

Arabelle opened the oven door
and watched the cake.
When she opened the door,
the cake was fat and tan
and filled the pan.
While she stood looking,
the cake
slowly
sank.

As she watched,
it turned into
a flat, wrinkled
failure.

Mrs. Mott came back
to the kitchen.
"What are you doing?" she asked.
"Watching the cake," said Arabelle.

"Oh, Arabelle. I didn't mean that.
You can't open the oven
while a cake is cooking,"
Mrs. Mott told her.

Arabelle took a deep breath,
but she did not yell
at her mother.
She only said,
"I can.
I am a failure."

Her mother took the pan
from the oven.

Her father
came into the kitchen.
He looked at the flat cake.
"What's that supposed to be?"

Arabelle ran to her room.

16

On a piece of cardboard,
she printed:

ARABELLE MOTT,
FAILURE

Mr. Mott was puzzled.
"Why does Arabelle run
when I ask a simple question?"
"Arabelle feels she's
a failure," Mrs. Mott said.
Mr. Mott was worried.
"She's not old enough
to be a failure."

He went to Arabelle's room

and made her invite him in.
"Why do you think
you're a failure?"
he wanted to know.

"I can't do anything right,"
she said.

"What do you like to do?"
her father asked.

"I like to do things right."

He thought for a while.
"What kind of things
do you like?"

"I like cake,
but I can't cook it right.
I like flowers,
but I can't paint them right."

20

"Why don't you *grow*
flowers then?"
he asked.
"All right," she said.
"I'll try anything."

Arabelle dug up
a bare corner
of the backyard.
She turned over the dirt
with a shovel.

She chopped the dirt fine
with a hoe.
She smoothed it flat
and soaked it.

Then she planted
poppy seeds,
pansy seeds,
carrot seeds,
tomato seeds,
some old bush bean seeds,
and the watermelon seeds
from her lunch.

Every day
she worked in her garden.
She promised
to give her friends
flowers
and melons
and vegetables.

They all came to see
her garden.

At last,
a green shoot came up.
Arabelle's friend Herman
pointed at it.
"What's that supposed to be?"

Arabelle got down
and looked at the shoot.
"A weed."
It looked so cheerful
she didn't have the heart
to pull it up.

"Weeds are all right,"
Herman said,
"but personally,
I'd rather eat watermelon."

Every day more weeds came up.
No flowers. No vegetables.
Just weeds.
Weeds and weeds.

Then, one day,
two different shoots came up.
"What are they supposed to be?"
Arabelle asked.
Her mother got down
and looked at the shoots.
"The big one
is a tomato vine,
and the little one
is a bush bean bush."

The next day
three carrot tops came up.

Arabelle worked even harder.
She watered her plants
and fed them.
She sang to them
and told them funny stories.

She promised all her friends
tomatoes
and carrots
and beans.

Her friend Linda
visited the garden.

Linda pointed at something
crawling on a tomato vine.
"What's that supposed to be?"

Arabelle got down
and looked at it.
"A snail.
It's eating my vine."

31

Linda shivered. "Ugh! Kill it!"
"It's only trying
to make a living."
Arabelle looked closer
at the snail.
"It has a nice face."

"I'm leaving
before it crawls
all over me," Linda said.

The next day
there were more snails
on Arabelle's vine.
"They seem to enjoy good food,"
she said.

Her friend Bosworth
was visiting her garden.
He pointed at a carrot top
that was moving.
"What's that supposed to be?"

The carrot top fell over.

Arabelle got down
and looked at the hole
where it had been.

A small
      gray
            furry
                  snout
wriggled once
and sank.

"A mole," Arabelle said.
"It took my carrot."

"Yuck!" Bosworth shuddered.
"Kill it."

"It's only trying
to eat right."

Arabelle looked
down the hole.
"It has a friendly snout."

"You are crazy," Bosworth said.
He went home.

Every day
another carrot fell over,
and a new hole
appeared in the garden.
More weeds came up.
More snails ate the vines.
Only the bush bean bush
had no problems.

Nobody came to see
Arabelle's garden
anymore.
Not many people liked bush beans.

Arabelle invited

her mother out
to visit the bean bush.
Her mother pointed
at a black bug
on the bush.
"What's that supposed to be?"

Arabelle looked closer
at the bug.
"I would say it's a beetle."

"What are you
going to do with it?"

Arabelle shrugged.
"Not many people like
bush beans anyway."

"Poor Arabelle," Mr. Mott said.
"Her garden is nothing
but weeds and snails
and beetles
and moles."

"I know." Mrs. Mott sighed.
"How can we get rid of them?"

"We'd better not.
They're all she has.
Without them, she'd only have
dirt."

"I hope our landlord
never sees
what a mess she's made,"
Mrs. Mott said.
"His little boy is
so neat."
Arabelle went on working
in her garden.

One day the landlord came.

He looked around the Motts'

living room.

He looked at the dirt

on Arabelle's jeans.

"What have you been doing

lately, Arabelle?"

he asked.

"I've been working in

my garden."

"I'm glad you're taking

good care of my yard,"

he said.

"What did you plant?"

"Fruit and flowers
and vegetables."

"I'd like to see them,"
he said.

Right away, Arabelle had a feeling
she should have kept
quiet.
"I don't think you would."
"Of course I would,"
he said.
"Show me your garden."

He followed Arabelle
out to the yard.
He looked at her garden.
"What a mess!"

Arabelle could tell
that he thought
she was a failure.
After all I have
been through, she decided
I will not
be a failure.
He frowned at the bush
covered with beetles.
"What's that supposed to be?"

Arabelle thought for a minute.
"That is my beetle bush.
I must have a hundred
healthy beetles
on that bush alone."

He bent down
to look at a
hole in the ground.
"What's that supposed to be?"

"My mole hole."

"You have a mole?" he asked.

"At least one," Arabelle said.
He pointed to
one of the shiny tracks
on the ground.
"What's that supposed to be?"

"My snail trail.
I probably have over five hundred
happy snails."

He picked up a can
full of black dots.
"What's this supposed to be?"

"My weed seed.
My weeds are so strong
I'm saving the seeds
to give people
who can't grow anything."

The landlord looked around him.
"What a mess!
What a wonderful mess."
He sat on the ground.
"Arabelle," he said,
"I am a failure as a father.
My backyard has
roses and fences
and perfect grass.

It has no weeds or snails or moles.
There's nothing going on
in my yard.
I don't believe
my child has ever seen
a beetle."

"He could come visit mine,"
Arabelle offered.

"You are a fine person,"
the landlord said.
Then he hurried away.

He came back with a boy
who was much younger
and cleaner
than Arabelle.
"This is a beetle bush,"
the landlord told him.

"Wow." The little boy looked
at the bush.

"And these are mole holes,"
the landlord said.
"A real mole
lives under there."

"Wow." The little boy
sat in the dirt.
"Over there," Arabelle said,
"are my snail trails."

The little boy
lay on his stomach
and turned his head
upside down
to look a snail in the eyes.

"If you like," Arabelle said,
"I can give you
some weed seed to take home."

The little boy
tied his weed seed
in his father's handkerchief.
"How do you grow snails
and beetles
and moles?" he asked.

"It's not hard," Arabelle told him.
"They just show up."

The little boy
pointed at something
behind a weed.

"What's that?"

The landlord separated the weeds.
"A watermelon.
You have a watermelon
hidden back here."

"I have?" Arabelle crawled
between the weeds.
She felt the melon all over.
She dusted it with a clean part
of her shirt.

Her parents and her friends
came to see it.

"That's the most beautiful melon
in the world," her mother said.

"How does it feel to be a success?"
her father asked.

"I don't know," Arabelle said.
"I'm still getting used to it."

That evening
she said good night
to the snails and moles.

She patted the beetle bush
and tucked the melon

back among the weeds.

She went to her room
and took down the sign
on her door.

Then she wrote a new poem:

Snails and moles
Are gentle souls.

Bugs and weeds
Have simple needs.

And all unwanted things, I know,
Are grateful for a place to grow.
So now that I am a success
I do not love them any less.

By Arabelle Mot
Ex-Failure